For Dan,

my treasured husband of 32 years

who walks God's wild woods with me.—S.R.

To my family, with love.—A.C.

WHO MADE THE WILD WOODS?

PUBLISHED BY WATERBROOK PRESS

5446 North Academy Boulevard, Suite 200

Colorado Springs, CO 80918

A division of Random House, Inc.

ISBN 1-57856-027-6

Printed in the United States of America

1999 — First Edition

10 9 8 7 6 5 4 3 2 1

WHO MADE THE

Wild Woods?

written by SCHARLOTTE RICH
art by ANNA CURREY

WATERBROOK
PRESS

WHO made the wildflowers that grow
in the woods? Yellow, blue, purple,
and pink! Tell me who made them?
Well, who do you think?

GOD made the wildflowers that grow
in the woods!
God is *so* good!

WHO made the white-footed mouse in the woods? She scurries to build her nest in the brush, jumping and looking for food in a rush.

She has babies to feed
so they won't fuss.

Did GOD make that mouse
with the furry white tummy?

Yes! GOD made the white-footed mouse
in the woods.
God made the wildflowers
with so many colors.

God is *so* good!

Then WHO made the birds
that sing in the woods? Chickadee,
sparrow, blue jay, and crow?
Tell me now, please!
Does any child know?

GOD made the birds that sing
   in the woods! God made the white-footed
mice that jump! God made the wildflowers
   with so many colors!

   God is *so* good!

WHO made the squirrels
   that hide nuts in the woods,
leaping and waving
   their big bushy tails?
Scurrying! Hurrying!
Oh, tell me, please,
before all that fur
   in the woods makes
me sneeze!

GOD made the squirrels
    with big bushy tails, and white-footed mice
        and birds that sing!
The Lord God made EVERYTHING!

WHO made the fox, so quiet and sly?
That bushy and furry and fast-running guy?
Just who made that fox?
Speak now or say why!

GOD made the furry
and fast-running fox!
God made the squirrels
that hide away nuts!
You don't have to think twice,
to know who made mice

and the birds and the flowers
   that grow deep in the woods!

God is *so* good!

But WHO made the skunk that digs
in the woods? Stinky-winky,
black and white, who hunts for
food in the bushes all night?
Please take a guess! Can it be that
you're right?

GOD made stinky-winky skunks,
furry foxes, scolding squirrels,
merry mice, beautiful birds,
and windblown wildflowers!

God is *so* good!

Well then, just WHO made
the porcupine that
    waddles in the woods?
So prickly and ickly,
    fat and slow?
        Come on! Think hard!
Well now, do you know?

GOD made prickly porcupines
that waddle in the woods!
God made stinky-winky skunks,
furry foxes, scolding squirrels,
merry mice, beautiful birds, and
windblown wildflowers!

God is *so* good!

WHO made the masked raccoons
    in the woods? Those stripe-tailed clowns
    in the old hollow tree? Such fine
    furry friends that hunt in the night?
I just know you will get this one right!

GOD made the masked raccoons
in the woods! God made the
prickly porcupine,
the stinky-winky skunk,
the fast-running fox,
the squirrels and the mice,

the birds that sing,
   and all the wildflowers
   with so many colors.

God is *so* good!

WHO made the deer that leap
in the woods? Brown-eyed and soft,
with white-spotted babies?
Who made the deer?
Now, who do you think?
Answer me, please,
as quick as a wink!

GOD made the deer
that leap in the woods!
God made raccoons,
porcupines,
skunks,
foxes, squirrels,
mice, birds,
and all the wildflowers
that grow in the woods!

God is *so* good!

WHO made the bear that sleeps
in the woods? Hunting for berries
and sweet honeycombs?
Who made the bear, so fat
with thick hair?
Can you answer my question?
Come on! Do you dare?

Oh yes, it's true!
God made bears and honey, too!

GOD made *everything*
in the woods!

God is *so* good!

But then...
WHO made the *children* that walk
in the woods?
Laughing and looking
at everything good,
loving and giving to everything living
deep in the woods?

Who made the children
and everything good?
GOD made the children
that walk in the woods!

God made
everything good!